Barbie as The Island Princess

Adapted by Judy Katschke
Based on the original screenpl...
by Cliff Ruby & Ela...

D1367512

Reader's Digest
Children's Books®

New York, New York • Montréal, Québec • Bath, United Kingdom

Once upon a time there was a sparkling tropical island. Many exotic birds and animals called the island home. So did an adventurous and beautiful girl named Ro.

Each day Ro gathered fruits with Sagi, the red panda. She also frolicked on the beach with Azul, the princely peacock, and swung on the vines with Tika, the baby elephant.

Ro loved her island. But she always had a feeling she belonged somewhere else.

One day, Ro and her family of friends spotted a great ship sailing into the cove.

On board were the handsome Prince Antonio and Frazer, the royal scientist. They couldn't wait to explore the magnificent island. But their hike through the jungle ended at a crocodile-filled swamp!

When Ro saw the fierce crocodiles snapping at the strangers, she ran to the rescue. "Riki, Taj, Kiki, that's enough!" she scolded them.

The crocodiles' jaws snapped shut. But Antonio's mouth opened with surprise. Who was this girl who could talk to animals?

"Sagi tells me I came from the sea a long time ago," Ro explained. She showed him a trunk—the only thing she had from her past.

"A shipwreck," Antonio guessed.

He invited Ro and her friends to visit his kingdom.

There she would meet more people—like herself! Ro
wished to find out where she came from.

    As the royal ship journeyed back toward Antonio's
kingdom of Appolonia, Ro and the prince fell in love.

Inside the castle, Ro met Antonio's parents, King Peter and Queen Danielle. She even chatted with Tallulah, the queen's pet monkey. But Ro wasn't the only surprise at the castle.

"Antonio, meet Princess Luciana, your beautiful bride-to-be," King Peter announced.

Ro didn't know Antonio was engaged. Neither

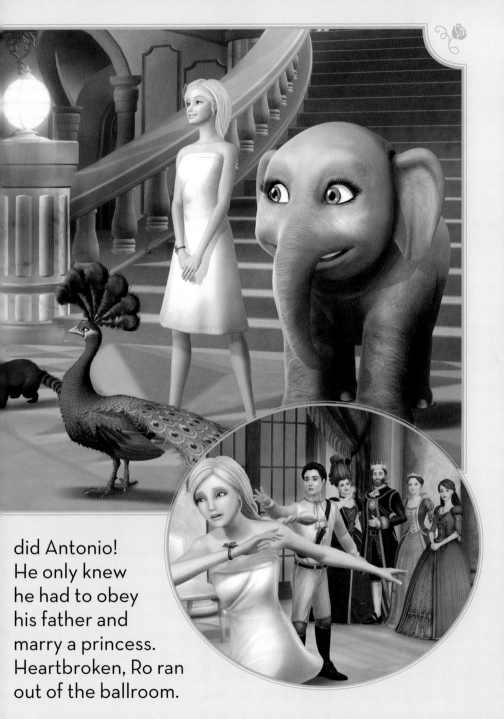

did Antonio!
He only knew
he had to obey
his father and
marry a princess.
Heartbroken, Ro ran
out of the ballroom.

Along with Luciana came her mother, Queen Ariana. Ariana was a wicked queen with a secret plan to destroy the royal family and rule the kingdom!

Ro was still sad about Antonio and Luciana, but Sagi, Azul, Tika, and Tallulah talked her into attending

the Royal Engagement Ball. They even made Ro a stunning blue gown adorned with peacock feathers. The dress was fit for a princess—an island princess!

Heads turned as the island girl swept into the ballroom. Antonio had never seen such a lovely sight.

He walked over to Ro and whispered, "May I have this dance?" Ro wanted to stay with Antonio forever. But she knew the prince had to marry a princess.

Meanwhile, Ariana plotted against Ro. She ordered her trusty rat servants to sprinkle sleeping powder in the food of every animal in the kingdom. By next morning, almost every animal was fast asleep, including Talullah! Ariana accused Ro of spreading the sickness. The King banished Ro and her friends from the kingdom, and put them on a boat heading back to their island.

Ro had to get back to the kingdom—she knew how to cure the sickness with roses from the castle greenhouse. She and her friends tried to escape from the boat, but were knocked into the sea.

As Ro struggled to stay afloat, a memory of her father's voice echoed through her head, "Don't give up, Rosella!" In a flash, she remembered her real name.

"Please help us, dolphins!" Ro cried. Ro and the others gratefully accepted a ride back to shore!

Ro wasted no time as she mixed the cure and gave it to the sleeping animals. As she did so, royal guards burst in to arrest her. She proclaimed her innocence.

No one believed Ro until a little bird told the truth: Ariana had poisoned the animals, not Ro!

"Ro, I knew you were innocent!" Antonio said.
Even King Peter apologized.

"Please call me Rosella, my real name," Ro said.

A beautiful woman named Queen Marissa
stepped forward. "I had a daughter named Rosella,"
she said. "She was lost at sea many years ago."

Sagi, Tika, and Azul sniffed back happy tears. If Ro's mother was a queen, that made Ro a princess!

Princess Rosella had found her mother at last. And as she stood with Prince Antonio on their wedding day, she knew she had found something just as wonderful—true love!